LIVING LANGUAGE®

Learn French in the Car

+ +

A PARENT–CHILD ACTIVITY KIT

Written by
Marie-Claire Antoine

Edited by
Helga Schier, Ph.D.

LIVING LANGUAGE®, A RANDOM HOUSE COMPANY
NEW YORK

Published by Living Language, A Random House Company, 201 East 50th Street, New York, New York 10022.
Random House, Inc. New York, Toronto, London, Sydney, Auckland
www.livinglanguage.com

Living Language is a registered trademark of Crown Publishers, Inc.

Printed in the United States of America

Design by Jesse Cohen

Library of Congress Cataloging-in-Publication Data
Antoine, Marie-Claire.
    Learn French in the car : a parent–child activity kit / written by Marie-Claire Antoine ; edited by Helga Schier.
    At head of title: Living Language (Living Language parent–child activity kit)
    1. French language—Textbooks for foreign speakers—English—Juvenile literature. 2. Games for travelers—
Juvenile literature. 3. Creative activities and seat work. I. Schier, Helga. II. Title. III. Series.
PC2129.E5A67   1998
448.3'421—dc21   97-47769

ISBN 0-609-60213-6
10   9   8   7   6   5   4   3   2   1
First Edition

Contents

Appendixes   40

Introduction

Living Language® Learn French in the Car is a fun and effective parent-child activity kit that teaches essential French vocabulary and phrases through sixteen exciting and easy-to-prepare activities centered around things you see on the road. Whether you already speak French and want your children to learn it, too, or whether you want to learn French along with your children, this program offers great educational fun and entertainment for the entire family. In Driver's Ed your kids will learn the French words for the road signs you'll pass; in Treasure Hunt they'll learn how to read maps; and the numbers on the license plates of passing cars will be used to play auto lotto in License Plates. *Bonne chance!*

The complete **Learn French in the Car** package includes this 48-page book and a 60-minute cassette.

The book comes complete with a step-by-step description of all the activities, a two-way glossary, a translation of the songs and rhymes used on the recordings, and one page of removable color stickers. At the beginning of each activity, carefully read the instructions with your children and gather all the materials necessary to complete the activity. During the activity, follow the step-by-step instructions carefully. Turn on the tape and listen as the two narrators guide you and your children through singing French folk songs, exercising at the rest stop to the rhythm of a French

rhyme, and playing a game of "I Spy" in French. Without even noticing it, you and your children will learn the most essential French words and phrases. Suggestions for adapting and modifying the activity to enhance learning conclude every activity.

The book doubles as a scrapbook that your children can personalize with drawings, photographs, or the included stickers to create a record of the completed activities.

The appendix features a two-way glossary that will prove to be an invaluable reference tool. In addition to all vocabulary used during the program, it includes several vocabulary lists, organized by topic, that go beyond the scope of this program.

The recordings feature vocabulary, phrases, songs, and rhymes, while the two narrators, Jacques and Jeannette, gently lead you and your children through each activity. They will teach the vocabulary and phrases and provide ample opportunity for you to practice your pronunciation. Just listen and repeat, and the French will easily roll off your tongue. French songs and rhymes help with learning. Don't worry if it seems difficult to follow the songs the first time around. Just rewind to listen to them again. For your convenience, transcriptions and translations of the songs and rhymes are included in the appendix at the back of this book.

And now, let's begin. *Commençons!*

Activities

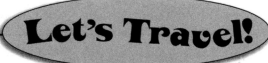
Time: 15 minutes

Vocabulary and Phrases
bonjour hello • *je m'appelle* my name is • *si j'étais* if I were • *le vélo* bicycle
la voiture car • *le bus* bus • *le bateau* boat • *l'avion* airplane • *le camion* truck
le taxi taxi • *un véhicule* a vehicle • *rapide* fast • *lent* slow

YOU NEED +

✔ a pen

+ +

1. Hello! Are you worried this car trip is going to be boring? Don't be! With **Learn French in the Car** you won't want to get out of the car. Not only will you get to play fun games, you will also learn to speak a new language: French. Are you ready? Let's start with a little game called If I Were . . .

2. The rule is simple. First, pick a partner. Then pretend to be a vehicle by announcing "If I were a vehicle, I would be . . ." and describe the type of vehicle you would be. For example, if you decide that you'd be a bicycle, you'd say that you have two wheels and a saddle. Without asking any questions, your partner must guess what you are.

3. To make this game even more interesting, let's play it in French. To learn your very first French words, turn on your **Learn French in the Car** tape now.

4. Remember all the French words you learned? Use as many of them as possible. Say *"Si j'étais un véhicule . . . "* (If I were a vehicle . . .). Your playmate should give the answer in French. Don't forget to take turns.

5. Here's a variation. Play the game as described, but instead of pretending to be just any vehicle, pretend to be a specific car. Say "If I were a car . . ." and describe what type of car you would be. Would you be a race car, or a convertible, or a jeep? Can you say "If I were a car . . ." in French?*

6. Now look on the right-hand page. See the drawings? Decide whether each vehicle pictured is fast or slow. For more fun, you can write your opinion next to each drawing. Can you say and write these two words in French? After that, look at the list of vehicles. Check "Yes" for all those you've already used. Otherwise check "No." Do you remember what some of them are called in French? Write their French names in the column provided.

*Answer: *Si j'étais une voiture . . .*

Let's Travel!

FAST or SLOW?

 _____    _____

 _____    _____

 _____   _____

Have you ever been in...

	Yes	No	En français . . .
a boat?	❏	❏	_____
a truck?	❏	❏	_____
a car?	❏	❏	_____
a covered wagon?	❏	❏	un chariot bâché
a bus?	❏	❏	_____
a plane?	❏	❏	_____
a taxi?	❏	❏	_____
a space shuttle?	❏	❏	une navette spatiale

My Car

Time: 20 minutes

Vocabulary and Phrases

la voiture car • *la roue* wheel • *le moteur* engine • *le phare* headlight
le volant steering wheel • *la porte* door • *l'antenne* antenna

YOU NEED ·

✔ stickers for *la roue* (wheel), *le phare* (headlight),
  l'antenne (antenna), *la porte* (door), *le moteur* (engine)
✔ a pen

· ·

1. Here's a fun activity that will teach you all you need to know about your car. Start by choosing a partner. Take turns naming five things each that are part of your car, inside, outside, or under the hood. Keep taking turns, until you run out of ideas. How long can you keep the game going?

2. Before you start, turn on the tape and listen to some new French words. They will help you play.

3. There's more to this game. First, give yourself five points for each thing you name. But if you name something in French, give yourself twenty points! Compete with your partner to get the most points. Careful: You can't both use the same words!

4. For a variation of the game, pick a "hot letter." What's that? That's a letter you're not allowed to pronounce. It can be part of the word, but you can't say it. For example: If your hot letter is "t," you'd say *"l'an-enne"* instead of *"l'antenne."* How do you choose a hot letter? Use the initial of your first name, or of your partner's first name. Then play the game as described above. If you pronounce the hot letter, deduct two points from your score. Don't forget: French words give you twenty points (but mind that hot letter!).

5. Now you know all about cars. So let's make sure that the car being built on the right-hand page is complete. On the engineer's notepad, you'll see a list of what's missing. Find the stickers that represent these things and put them in the right place.

At the car factory

We need:

LA ROUE
LE PHARE
L'ANTENNE
LA PORTE
LE MOTEUR

Animal Spotting

Time: 5, 10, or 15 minutes

Vocabulary and Phrases
la voiture car • *la vache* cow • *le cheval* horse • *le mouton* sheep
le chien dog • *l'oiseau* bird

YOU NEED +

✔ stickers with *le cheval* (horse), *la vache* (cow),
   le mouton (sheep), *le chien* (dog), *l'oiseau* (bird)
✔ a pen

+ +

1. You are traveling by car today. Where are you going? To Grandma's? To a theme park? In any case, you must be impatient to get there. Here's a fun game that will make the trip seem shorter. It's called Animal Spotting. How do you play? That's easy. Look out the car window and watch for animals. For each animal you see, you score points. If you see a sheep, you get five points; for a horse you get four points; for a cow you get three points; for a dog two points; and for a bird one point. Spot any other animal and you get a six-point bonus! The winner is the player who reaches a total of thirty points first. As soon as you see an animal, you must say so.

2. Only the player to spot an animal first gets the points. Just say "Cow!" or "Horse!" and score. If you see more than one animal at once, double the corresponding number of points. For example, if you see a herd of eight cows grazing, count six points.

3. Before you start playing, turn on the tape to learn the French names of the animals we're looking for.

4. Okay, let's start! Remember that you need at least thirty points to win. To increase the challenge, use your new French words to announce the animals you see.

5. You can also add some variation to Animal Spotting. If there aren't a lot of animals by the side of the road, set a time limit instead of a high score. With your partners, play for five, ten, or fifteen minutes. The player who collects the highest number of points during that time wins the game.

6. You want to play, but you can't see any animals at the moment? Perhaps you are driving in a city or through a tunnel. Be patient. In the meantime, turn on the tape again to learn a fun song: *Jacques et Jeannette ont une ferme* (Jacques and Jeannette Have a Farm).

7. Look at the animals on the right-hand page. Do you remember what they are called in French? Look for the correct stickers and match them with the drawings.

8. Do you like to draw? Use the blank space at the bottom of the page to draw two animals you would find on a farm. Do you know their names in French? What sounds do they make?

What animals are these?

My two favorite farm animals

Map and Navigation

Time: 15 minutes

Vocabulary and Phrases

va go • *à droite* to the right • *à gauche* to the left
tout droit straight ahead • *en arrière* at the back • *la direction* direction

YOU NEED ✦✦

✔ a road map
✔ a pen

✦✦

1. When you are traveling to a new place, how do you find your way? Right, you use a road map. Do you have one in the car? Great! Let's play with it. First, choose a partner. Imagine you are explorers. You are the navigator and your partner is the pilot. Your role is to read the map and guide your partner.

2. Choose a departure point on the map: It could be your hometown or the last city you passed. After that, secretly pick a destination, which is also on the map. The destination can be a city, a forest, a mountain . . . anything that appeals to you.

3. Now guide your partner from the departure point to your secret destination. Give directions (to the right, to the left, straight ahead, back) while you both look at the map. Your partner will follow the way on the map according to your instructions. When you stop giving directions, your partner will name the place he or she has reached on the map. Is it your secret destination? If so, switch roles. If not, keep going.

4. Before you start exploring, turn on the tape and learn how to give directions in French.

5. Now that you know the important French phrases, start your game. Pretend you are an explorer from France and guide your partner in French.

6. You don't have a map? Or you want more fun but don't want to use the map? Well, let's play Where? Quickly name things you are seeing outside the car window. As you name each thing, your partner will look and say whether you're seeing it to the right, to the left, straight ahead, or behind the car. The faster you name things, the faster your partner has to look and say where those things are. Switch roles when your partner makes a mistake. To make the game more exciting, use the French expressions *à droite* (to the right), *à gauche* (to the left), *tout droit* (straight ahead), and *en arrière* (at the back, behind).

7. Still more fun! Look at the right-hand page. Do you see all those tangled lines? Only one leads from your house to Disneyland. Which one?

Time: 45 minutes

Vocabulary and Phrases

j'arrête I stop • *j'avance* I go forward • *je tourne* I turn (I make a turn) • *je ralentis* I slow down
je mets le clignotant I put the blinker on • *je double* I pass • *je ne peux pas doubler* I can't pass

YOU NEED

✔ stickers with a stop sign, a deer crossing sign, a speed limit sign
✔ a pen

1. Will you learn to drive when you're older? Why not get a head start now? Imagine that you are the driver of your car at this moment. You must pay attention to what's happening on the road and respect the traffic signs. Say which driving decision you make each time you see an actual sign or change on the road. For example, if you see a stop sign, say: "I stop." Or if you see a straight dividing line, say: "I can't pass."

2. Before you "take the wheel," turn on the tape to learn some French driving expressions.

3. To make the game more exciting, pretend you are driving in France and use the French expressions you have just learned.

4. You can even be a driving instructor. Choose a partner to be your student, then invent a driving situation for him or her. Your partner will describe what he or she decides to do and mime driving accordingly. For example, say there's a right turn. You partner will answer "I turn" and mime turning the wheel. Watch your partner!

As the instructor, you must catch all the mistakes. Did your student use the blinker? Switch roles after each situation. One more thing: the student is French, so remind your partner to use as many French expressions as possible.

5. Have you noticed any yellow signs along your way? These are warning signs. They may show a picture of men working or children crossing. Look at the right-hand page. See the three blank signs? Read their meaning and invent a picture for each. Be creative!

6. What type of driver would you be? Quick, do the personality test on the right-hand page to find out! Check *Oui* (Yes) or *Non* (No) depending on your answer, then read the results. Do you agree with them?

7. More fun? No problem! Find the stickers that represent the road signs described and put them in the correct space. What would you do if you saw each sign while driving? Can you say it in French?

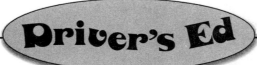

Silly Signs

Draw each sign according to the meaning given.

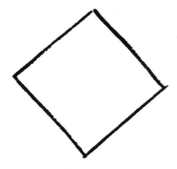 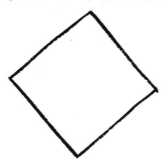 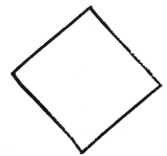

Santa Crossing   **T-Rex Playing**   **Easter Bunny Working**

Speed Limit: 50   **Stop**   **Deer Crossing**

What type of driver would you be?

		Oui	*Non*
1.	The traffic light turns yellow. You stop.	❏	❏
2.	You put the blinker on before making a left turn.	❏	❏
3.	You slow down when you see the sign Men at Work.	❏	❏
4.	You respect the speed limit.	❏	❏
5.	You keep a spare tire in the trunk.	❏	❏

You have a majority of *Oui*. Wonderful! Prudent and aware, you would be a great driver. Your friends would feel safe riding with you!

You have a majority of *Non*. Well, it's a good thing you're not driving yet! Make sure you learn all the safety rules before you start driving!

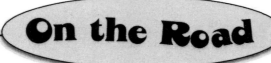

On the Road

Time: 30 minutes

Vocabulary and Phrases

la ville city • *l'école* school • *le parc* park • *le zoo* zoo • *la maison* house • *l'hôtel* hotel
la piscine swimming pool • *le magasin* shop

YOU NEED ++

✔ a pen

++

1. What do towns have in common? Each town has houses, schools, and hotels or motels to greet travelers like you. Why not use these places in a game? How? Mime them! First, pick a partner. Then pick one place from the list below. That done, mime what people do there. Act several roles if you need to. For example, if you choose to mime a school, you can mime the teacher and the students. Your partner has to guess which place you chose. He or she will give you the answer in French.

2. Turn on the tape now so you both can learn the French terms. Here is the list of place names to choose from:

le parc (park) *l'hôtel* (hotel)
le magasin (shop) *la maison* (house)
le zoo (zoo) *la piscine* (swimming pool)
l'école (school)

Now, you're ready to play!

3. Here's a variation. Pick a word from the list and say it to your partner. He or she must then mime what one person would be doing there, and you have to guess who this person is. For example, if you pick *le magasin* your partner might mime the salesperson or the customer.

4. Would you like to sing and mime *Sur le pont d'Avignon* (On the Avignon Bridge), a French folk song? Turn on the tape now.

5. Look at the right-hand page. Do you remember what these French words mean? Fill in the crossword puzzle with their English equivalents (we wrote in one word as an example). When you're finished, the name of a fun place will appear.

6. Now look at the street signs. Their letters got all mixed up by a tornado! Can you put each French word in the right order?

18

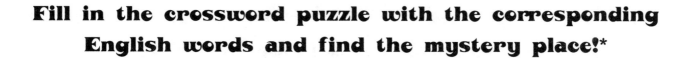

On the Road

Fill in the crossword puzzle with the corresponding English words and find the mystery place!*

1. école
2. piscine
3. parc
4. ville
5. maison
6. magasin

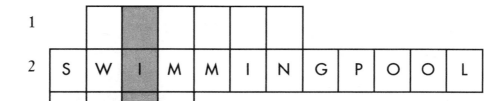

Row 2: S W I M M I N G P O O L

JUMBLE! Unscramble these city signs.†

CELOÉ

SANGIMA

LTÔHE

ACPR

*Answer: circus.
†Answer: école, magasin, hôtel, parc.

I'm Hungry!

Time: 25 minutes

Vocabulary and Phrases

j'ai faim I'm hungry • *je mange* I eat • *Est-ce que c'est . . . ?* Is it . . . ? • *oui* yes • *non* no
un légume a vegetable • *la viande* meat • *un fruit* a fruit • *un plat de fast-food* a fast-food dish
un dessert a dessert • *une glace* an ice-cream • *un gâteau* a cake

YOU NEED +

    ✔ **a pen**

+ +

1. Are you hungry? What would you like to eat? Let's play food riddles and let your playmates guess. The game is very simple. Pick something you'd like to eat and have your partner guess what it is. Your partner can ask you up to five questions. After that, he or she must guess what you chose. If your partner guesses right, switch roles. *Attention!* Answer the questions only with *oui* or *non.* Do you remember what those words mean? They mean "yes" and "no."

2. Your partner can use some French expressions too. As a matter of fact, each time he or she asks you a question in French, he or she gets an extra guess at the end. So quick, turn on the tape to learn some food-related expressions.

3. Are you ready? Great! Don't forget to switch roles whenever your partner guesses right. Remember to ask *Est-ce que c'est un(e) . . . ?* (Is it a . . . ?). For example: *Est-ce que c'est un gâteau?* (Is it a cake?).

4. Would you like to play another fun food game? Then start by reading this list of food categories:

- *les légumes* (vegetables)
- *la viande* (meat)
- *les desserts* (desserts)
- *les fruits* (fruits)
- *les plats de fast-food* (fast-food dishes)

Choose one category and name as many foods as possible that belong to it. As soon as you can't think of another name, the next player takes over. Keep taking turns until everybody runs out of ideas for the category. Can you name some foods in French? Can you say the category in French, too?

5. Look at the right-hand page. How do you feel about each of the foods pictured? Draw a "yummy" sign ☺ if you like that food, or a "yuck" sign ☹ if you don't. When you're finished, write the name of the category each food belongs to (fruits, vegetables, meat, etc.). Can you write the categories in French?

6. Imagine you are dining in a French restaurant. After the meal, the waiter brings you the dessert menu. But something is wrong! Read the menu and cross out everything that is not a dessert.

Yummy **or Yuck** **?**

 _____

 _____

 _____

 _____

 _____

 _____

 _____

 _____

 _____

 _____

 _____

_____

Dessert time!

Cross out everything that is not a dessert.

Les Desserts

Le Taco   L'Orange

La Salade de Fruits

Le Hot Dog

La Glace   Le Gateau

La Pizza   Le Hamburger

Time: 15 minutes

Vocabulary and Phrases

Jacques a dit Simon Says (lit., Jacques said) • *Dansez!* Dance! • *Marchez!* Walk! • *Tournez!* Turn!
Sautez! Jump! • *Reculez!* Walk back! • *Levez le bras!* Raise your arm!
Levez la jambe! Raise your leg! • *Applaudissez!* Applaud!

YOU NEED ··

✔ **a pen**

···

1. Rest stops are a fun part of the trip. You get to stretch your legs and play. Here's a way to take advantage of that time out of the car: Play Simon Says. Do you know this game? First, you need at least one partner. Then choose a game leader. The game leader says "Simon says . . ." and gives a command, such as "Dance!" The players must obey and dance. If the game leader gives a command without saying "Simon says" first, the players must not move. If they do, they're out of the game!

2. Now, why don't you make this game more challenging by playing it in French? Turn on the tape now to learn the words you will need.

3. Are you ready? Good. Give your first command in French. Of course, you can give commands in English, but try to use as many as possible in your new language. Remember: Move only if you hear *Jacques a dit* . . . (Simon Says . . .).

4. How about another game with French commands? Let's play Freeze! In this version, the game leader turns his or her back to the players and gives a command. The players do what they're asked. But as soon as the game leader turns around, they must freeze in whatever position they are in. The first player to move loses.

5. Congratulations! You just got a job at the circus. You are now the elephant trainer. Look at each illustration on the right-hand page. See what the elephant is doing? That's what you ordered him to do. Can you write in each command in French? (We wrote one in as an example.)

The ELEPHANT

DANSEZ!

_____

_____

_____

_____

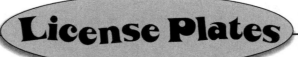

License Plates

Time: 10 minutes

Vocabulary and Phrases

un, deux, trois, quatre, cinq one, two, three, four, five
six, sept, huit, neuf, dix six, seven, eight, nine, ten

YOU NEED ∙∙

✔ a pen

∙∙∙

1. Numbers are written all over your car. They're on the dashboard dials, the radio display, the license plates. Let's play with them. Auto Lotto is like a regular game of lotto, only the numbers you pick must appear on a license plate. Pick three numbers between 1 and 9. Say them out loud, so your parent will know what they are. If two people are playing, it's okay to pick one or two numbers that are the same.

2. For more fun, say your numbers in French. Turn on the tape to learn how to do that.

3. You or your parent will read the license plate of the next car that passes. How many of your numbers are on it? If your three numbers are part of the car's license plate, you win the jackpot! If there are several players, the winner is the one who picked the most numbers on the license plate.

4. Do you want to keep playing with license plates? Look for your birthday! See if your month and date of birth appear on a plate. The player whose birthday appears first wins! And, of course, you can say each number one by one in French.

5. Now look at the right-hand page. One of the numbers in the box is the magic number. To find it, cross out all the numbers that appear more than once. The magic number is the last one left. How do you say that magic number in French?

6. In the blank box, draw the license plate of your car. Don't forget the symbol for your state!

Magic number

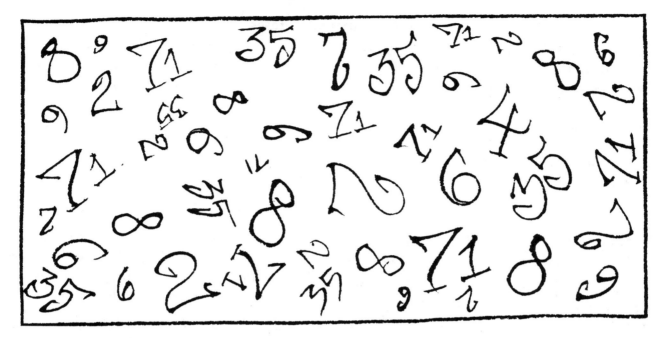

My license plate

Time: 15 minutes

Vocabulary and Phrases

je chante I sing • *je vais* I'm going • *je vais en voyage* I'm going on a trip • *la chanson* song
chanter to sing • *le chanteur* singer (male) • *la chanteuse* singer (female) • *le voyage* trip
papa dad • *maman* mom • *mon frère* my brother • *ma soeur* my sister • *la famille* family

YOU NEED

✔ music award sticker
✔ a pen

1. Do you like to sing? Great! Let's play Karaoke. Simply sing along with your **Learn French in the Car** tape.

2. First, listen to our song. It's called *Au clair de la lune* (In the Moonlight). Quick, turn on the tape to learn the words!

3. Now play *Au clair de la lune* again and sing along. After ten seconds, your parent will turn off the sound (but not the tape). Keep singing! After a few phrases, your parent will turn the sound back on. Are you at the same place as Jacques? Did you sing too fast or too slow? If so, try again.

4. Win a music award! Look for the music award sticker at the end of the book. Then take turns with your playmates singing *Au clair de la lune* on your own, without the tape. Your parent will decide who gave the best performance and award the music award sticker to the winner.

5. Now, be a composer. Create a little rap song about your car trip. How? Turn on the tape again. You'll learn a few words you could use in your song and hear an example.

6. Ready? Try to use as many French words as you can in your song. For help, scan this book to find words you've already learned.

7. Now look at the right-hand page. See the letters on the Word Scramble tiles? Which French words can you make with these letters? Here's a hint: You can make four words, all related to the French word for "song."*

8. Finally, draw your family. When you're done, label each person. Can you label everybody in French?

*Answer: chanson, chanter, chanteur, chanteuse

Word Scramble

My family

Wild Nature

Time: 30 minutes

Vocabulary and Phrases

la nature nature • *le cerf* deer • *la forêt* forest • *l'arbre* tree
l'animal animal • *le serpent* snake • *le désert* desert • *l'ours* bear • *l'aigle* eagle
la montagne mountain • *le requin* shark • *l'océan* ocean • *le lion* lion • *la jungle* jungle

YOU NEED

✔ stickers for *l'océan* (ocean), *la montagne* (mountain), *la forêt* (forest),
  l'arbre (tree), *la jungle* (jungle)
✔ a pen

1. Are you traveling through a forest? Passing through a desert? Maybe you are rolling up and down mountains or hills? In any case, there are certainly many wild animals living nearby—perhaps big bears or snakes. Even in the city, there are wild animals. Where? At the zoo, of course! Here's a fun game to play. It's called Animal Charades. It's simple. Mime a wild animal and your partner guesses which one it is.

2. First, decide which wild animal you will mime. Then tell your partner where this animal lives. For example, does it live in the ocean or in the jungle? After giving the clue, don't make another sound. Start miming the animal you chose, using only your face and hands. Take turns with your partner after he or she gives the right answer. If you have several playmates, the next turn belongs to the player who first guesses correctly.

3. For even more fun, you can give the clue in French. How? Well, first you need to turn on the tape to learn the French words.

4. If you get tired of being silent, you can imitate the sound of an animal instead of miming it. Give the clue as explained above and start growling, roaring, or whatever. But try not to be too loud!

5. After playing Animal Charades, why not sing a song? *La mère Michel* (Mother Michael) is a well-known French folk song. Turn on the tape again.

6. Look at the animals on the right-hand page. Find the stickers that tell where they live in French, and match them with each drawing.

7. Go on a paper safari. Each time you see an animal, write its French name on the right-hand page, draw it, and note in French where it lives and what it eats. Which one would you prefer as a pet? What do your parents think about that?

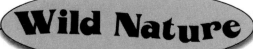

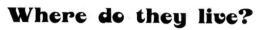

Where do they live?

Paper Safari

Animal I saw	Where it lives	What it eats

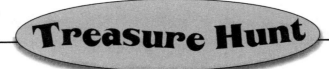

Treasure Hunt

Time: 10 minutes

Vocabulary and Phrases

j'ai I have • *tu as* you have • *la cassette* cassette • *le mouchoir* handkerchief
les lunettes de soleil sunglasses • *le chapeau* hat • *le stylo* pen • *le jouet* toy • *le jeu vidéo* video game
la carte map • *le livre* book • *la pièce* coin

YOU NEED +

✔ a pen

+ +

1. Are you tired of looking out the window? Well then, look in the car! There's nothing to see? Not so! There are even enough things for you to go on a treasure hunt.

2. The principle of the game is simple. First, choose a partner. Then compete to find as many objects as possible within a short time limit. The objects you need to find are listed below. But first, turn on the tape to learn how to say these words in French.

3. Ready? Here is the list of things you must find:

   le mouchoir (handkerchief)
   le jeu vidéo (video game)
   le chapeau (hat)
   les lunettes de soleil (sunglasses)
   la cassette (cassette)
   le livre (book)
   la pièce (coin)
   le stylo (pen)
   la carte (map)
   le jouet (toy)

4. You have five minutes to collect as many of the objects as possible. The first player who sees an object gets it. Your parent can act as a referee in case of disagreement. After five minutes, your parent will tell you to stop. The winner is the player who has collected everything, or the player who has the most points. Count ten points for each object you have. If you name an object in French, count twenty points! Even with fewer objects, you could still win if you speak more French than your partner does!

5. Look at the maze on the right-hand page. Can you find the way to the treasure? Look at the objects you pass on your way. Can you give their names in French?

City Spy

Time: 10 minutes

Vocabulary and Phrases

je vois I see • *quelque chose* something • *qui commence par* that starts with
l'alphabet français the French alphabet

YOU NEED •

✔ stickers with the letters A, V, G, O, P, R, T, W, E, H
✔ a pen

• •

1. Are you passing through a city? Wonderful! It's the perfect place to play I Spy. First, look out the window and pick something you are seeing at the moment. Don't tell what it is. Just say "I spy something that starts with . . ." and give the first letter of the word. Your partner then tries to figure out what you spied. He or she will look only for things that start with the letter you gave. When he or she has found it, switch roles.

2. Do you have your spy sunglasses on? Great! To make the game more challenging, give the first letter of the thing you spy in French. Turn on the tape now to learn the French alphabet.

3. Now you're ready. Do you remember how to say "I see something that starts with . . . ?" You say: "*Je vois quelque chose qui commence par . . .*"

4. Of course, you don't have to be in a city to play. You can choose something you are seeing on the road, in the car, or even in the car behind you.

5. The French alphabet can also become a secret spy code: Use it to spell secret words to your partner. And if you'd like to learn a fun alphabet poem called *L'alphabet, c'est rhymé* (The Alphabet, It Rhymes), turn on the tape again.

6. Look on the right-hand page. See the message? It's top secret! Some letters have been erased by accident. Find the stickers with the letters to complete and read this very important message. When you're finished, look at the second message. It's coded. To read it, write the letters that correspond to each number. Can you say those letters in French?

Top Secret!

Complete the message with the stickers of the missing letters.

DEAR AGENT 807:

I WILL BE GOING ON A TRIP NEXT SATURD_____Y. I WILL LEA_____E EARLY

IN THE MORNIN_____. PLEASE, MAKE SURE YOU GO TO MY H_____USE.

(YOU KNOW WHERE IT IS.) MY PET FISH NEEDS TO BE FED. I KNOW YOU

ARE WORRIED BECAUSE MY _____ET IS A BIG SHA_____K, BUT "TOOTSIE"

IS VERY GENTLE. JUST BE CAREFUL WHEN YOU PU_____YOUR HAND IN

THE _____ATER! I WILL RETURN NEXT W_____DNESDAY. T_____ANK

YOU FOR YOUR HELP.

P.S. TOOTSIE IS IMPATIENT TO SEE YOU!

AGENT 000

Break the code! Write the corresponding letter under each number.

15.4.10.11.10 1.11.10 24.1.2.7 15.4.9.2.14.17 15.21 17.10.10 9.2 1 13.9.15.7

26.18.15 15.4.10 25.9.5.6.10.17.15 8.5.1.13.10 9.17 15.4.10 22.21.21!

Secret code

A=1 B=26 C=13 D=6 E=10 F=19 G=14 H=4 I=9 J=20 K=16 L=5 M=24

N=2 O=21 P=8 Q=23 R=11 S=17 T=15 U=18 V=12 W=25 X=3 Y=7 Z=22

Colors

Time: 20 minutes

Vocabulary and Phrases

la couleur color • *rouge* red • *blanc* white • *bleu* blue • *orange* orange • *gris* gray • *jaune* yellow
vert green • *rose* pink • *violet* purple • *noir* black • *marron* brown

YOU NEED

✔ stickers for *rouge* (red), *bleu* (blue), *vert* (green), *jaune* (yellow)
✔ a pen

1. Doesn't the road look like a rainbow with all these colorful cars and trucks? Here's a rainbow of activities called Color Me. First, choose a partner. Tell him or her: Color me . . . and give a color of your choice—in French! Your partner has to name as many things as possible of that color. For example, suppose you say "Color me *vert*" (green). You partner might answer: "grass, a frog, leaves, my uncle's car, my friend Annie's eyes, my favorite T-shirt, my school bag," and so on, until he or she can't think of anything else that's green. At that point, switch roles. Your partner will choose a new color in French for you. Who will give the longest answer?

2. Before you find out, turn on the tape so you can learn the French names of the colors and a fun poem called *Les couleurs de l'univers* (The Colors of the Universe).

3. Are you up for a challenge? Choose a color as above, but name only things of that color you are actually seeing out of the car window. Compete with your partner by keeping score, counting ten points for each thing you name.

4. Here's another colorful idea. Name the colors of the next ten cars you pass. Compete with your partner to announce the color first. Can you name the colors in French? The player who gives the most color names in French becomes the Rainbow Master.

5. More fun? Pretend you are exploring a new planet. It's very much like Earth, except the colors are different. For example, the sky is red and the grass is purple. Can you imagine that new planet? Imagine the color of its ocean, trees, mountains, sun, moon, snow . . . and everything else you can think of. Be creative! And since you're on a foreign planet, why not use a foreign language? Can you say some of the colors in French?

6. Now look at the right-hand page. Imagine that you've found old black-and-white pictures. Read what each picture represents, then place the sticker with the name of its color next to it. When you're finished, answer the questions about your favorite colors. Can you write some answers in French?

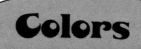

What color is each picture?

Bananas

Fire truck

Ocean

Prairie

What color is...

your favorite T-shirt? _____   your favorite hat? _____

your car? _____   your school bag? _____

My favorite color is _____.

My least favorite color is _____.

Every Day's a Holiday!

Time: 10 minutes

Vocabulary and Phrases

aujourd'hui c'est . . . today is . . . • *aujourd'hui* today • *le jour* day
lundi Monday • *mardi* Tuesday • *mercredi* Wednesday • *jeudi* Thursday
vendredi Friday • *samedi* Saturday • *dimanche* Sunday

YOU NEED ·

✔ stickers for *lundi* (Monday), *mardi* (Tuesday), *mercredi* (Wednesday), *jeudi* (Thursday), *vendredi* (Friday), *samedi* (Saturday), *dimanche* (Sunday)

✔ a pen

· ·

1. What day is today? What did you do yesterday? What are your plans for tomorrow? Turn on the tape to learn what the days are called in French.

2. This game will take you into the past, present, and future. Let's start with today's day. Give it in French. Now think of what happened today and name someone you met, something that you ate, something you read, something you played, and something you're wearing.

3. Good! Now do the same thing for yesterday. Give yesterday's day in French, then name someone you met, something you ate, something you read, something you played, and something you wore.

4. That was the present and the past. Can you predict the future? Say what day tomorrow will be and name who you will meet and what you will eat, read, play, and wear. Can you go further into the future and predict those things for the next weekend? Don't forget to give the name of each day in French!

5. Now look on the right-hand page. There's a calendar that looks very empty. Imagine each day is a holiday. First, find the stickers with the days of the week in French and place them over the corresponding English days. Then, for each day, write or draw what you would like to do in the morning and in the afternoon. Think of all the things you like to do when you're having a holiday. Have fun!

My Holiday Calendar

	MORNING	AFTERNOON
MONDAY		
TUESDAY		
WEDNESDAY		
THURSDAY		
FRIDAY		
SATURDAY		
SUNDAY		

Time: 20 minutes

Vocabulary and Phrases

quelque chose something • *c'est* it's • *amusant* fun • *ennuyeux* boring • *long* long • *court* short
étrange strange • *beau* beautiful • *laid* ugly • *grand* big • *petit* small

YOU NEED •

   ✔ **a pen**

• •

1. Is your trip almost over? Here's an activity that will help you remember it. Can you remember what you've seen on the way? Can you say if it was fun, boring, or even strange? That's what you'll do with this game.

2. Turn on the tape to learn how to describe things in French.

3. Pick a partner. Ask him or her one of the questions from the list below. Say:
"Name . . ."

- *quelque chose de grand* (something big)
- *quelque chose de petit* (something small)
- *quelque chose d'amusant* (something fun)
- *quelque chose d'ennuyeux* (something boring)
- *quelque chose de laid* (something ugly)
- *quelque chose de beau* (something beautiful)
- *quelque chose d'étrange* (something strange)

Your partner has to name two things he or she saw during the trip that correspond to what you asked. For example, you may ask: "Name *quelque chose de grand.*" He or she might answer: "A mountain and the bridge we just passed."

4. Switch roles after each question. Keep score. How? Count ten points for each answer. If you read the question in French, add twenty points to your score. Keep playing until you run out of ideas and can't answer any of the questions. The player who has the most points is the winner.

5. Another challenge? Can you give some of the answers in French? If so, count fifty points for each. To help you, look for French words all through this book.

6. Look on the right-hand page. There's a secret message hidden in the puzzle. To discover it, find all the listed words in the puzzle. Make sure you look carefully in all directions. When you're done, write all the unused letters and read the message!

7. So, how was your trip? Was it fun? Boring? Short? Long? Circle the words that match your opinion, and cross out the others. Look at the words you've circled. Do you remember how to say them in French?

Word Search

All these words are in the puzzle. To find them, look from right to left, left to right, up, down, and diagonally. When you have found all the words, write the remaining unused letters from left to right and see a secret message appear!

B	H	B	D	R	I	V	I	N	G
U	I	A	I	R	P	L	A	N	E
S	N	C	A	B	P	P	I	R	T
U	I	K	Y	P	O	M	Y	R	H
N	A	P	H	C	O	A	L	O	G
T	R	A	V	E	L	C	T	A	I
A	T	C	A	R	D	E	M	D	A
N	Y	K	T	O	L	E	Y	O	U

AIRPLANE
BACKPACK
BICYCLE
BOAT
BUS
CAMP
CAR
DRIVING

GAME
HOTEL
ROAD
SUNTAN
TRAIN
TRAVEL
TRIP

The secret message is: _____.

My trip was...

boring   fun
short   long
strange   beautiful

Appendixes

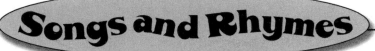

JACQUES ET JEANNETTE ONT UNE FERME

Jacques et Jeannette ont une ferme,
tra-la-la-la-la.
Et dans leur ferme ils ont une vache,
tra-la-la-la-la.
La vache dit meuh meuh
Et meuh meuh meuh.
Elle dit meuh, répète meuh.
Elle dit toujours meuh!

Jacques et Jeannette ont une ferme
tra-la-la-la-la.
Et dans leur ferme ils ont un mouton,
tra-la-la-la-la.
Le mouton dit bêh-bêh
et bêh-bêh-bêh.
Il dit bêh, répète bêh.
Il dit toujours bêh!

Jacques et Jeannette ont une ferme
tra-la-la-la-la.
Et dans leur ferme ils ont un chien,
tra-la-la-la-la.
Le chien dit wouf-wouf
et wouf-wouf-wouf.
Il dit wouf, répète wouf.
Il dit toujours wouf!

JACQUES AND JEANNETTE HAVE A FARM

Jacques and Jeannette have a farm,
tra-la-la-la-la.
And on their farm they have a cow,
tra-la-la-la-la.
The cow says moo moo
And moo moo moo.
It says moo, repeats moo.
It always says moo!

Jacques and Jeannette have a farm
tra-la-la-la-la.
And on their farm they have a sheep,
tra-la-la-la-la.
The sheep says bah-bah
and bah-bah-bah.
It says bah, repeats bah.
It always says bah!

Jacques and Jeannette have a farm
tra-la-la-la-la.
And on their farm they have a dog,
tra-la-la-la-la.
The dog says bow-wow
and bow-wow-bow-wow.
It says bow-wow, repeats bow-wow.
It always says bow-wow!

SUR LE PONT D'AVIGNON

Sur le pont d'Avignon,
l'on y danse, l'on y danse.
Sur le pont d'Avignon,
l'on y danse tout en rond.
Les beaux messieux font comme ça.
Et puis encore comme ça.
Les belles dames font comme ça.
Et puis encore comme ça.
Sur le pont d'Avignon,
l'on y danse, l'on y danse.
Sur le pont d'Avignon,
l'on y danse tout en rond.

AU CLAIR DE LA LUNE

Au clair de la lune, mon ami Pierrot,
Prête-moi ta plume, pour écrire
   un mot.
Ma chandelle est morte, je n'ai plus de feu.
Ouvre-moi ta porte, pour l'amour de Dieu.

Au clair de la lune, Pierrot répondit:
Je n'ai pas de plume, je suis dans mon lit.
Va chez la voisine, je crois qu'elle y est.
Car dans sa cuisine, on bat le briquet.

LA MÈRE MICHEL

C'est la mère Michel qui a perdu son chat,
Qui crie par la fenêtre à qui le lui rendra.
C'est le père Lustucru qui lui a répondu:
Allez, la mère Michel, votre chat n'est pas perdu.

Sur l'air du tra la la la,
Sur l'air du tra la la la.
Sur l'air du tra dé ri dé ra et tra la la.

ON THE AVIGNON BRIDGE

On the Avignon bridge,
we are dancing, we are dancing.
On the Avignon bridge,
we are dancing in a circle.
The gentlemen move like that.
And again like that.
The pretty ladies move like that.
And again like that.
On the Avignon bridge,
we are dancing, we are dancing.
On the Avignon bridge,
we are dancing in a circle.

IN THE MOONLIGHT

In the moonlight, my friend Pierrot,
Lend me your quill pen, so I can write
   a note.
My candle has died, I have no light left.
Open your door, for goodness' sake.

In the moonlight, Pierrot answered:
I have no quill pen, I am in my bed.
Go see the neighbor, I think she's home.
Because in her kitchen, someone's
   striking a light.

MOTHER MICHAEL

Mother Michael has lost her cat,
She shouts out the window to get it back.
It was Father Lustucru who answered her:
Come on, Mother Michael, your cat
   isn't lost.
To the tune of tra la la la,
To the tune of tra la la la.
To the tune of tra dé ri dé ra and tra la la.

L'ALPHABET, C'EST RHYMÉ

A, B, C, c'est assez.
D, E, F, c'est trop bref.
G, H, I, c'est petit.
J, K, L, c'est pêle-mêle.
M, N, O, c'est nouveau.
P, Q, R, c'est super.
S, T, U, c'est connu.
V, W, c'est rêvé.
X, Y, c'est du grec.
Et le Z, c'est un zèbre!

LES COULEURS DE L'UNIVERS

Les couleurs de l'univers
La planète Terre est bleue.
La planète Mars est rouge.
La planète Jupiter est orange.
La lune est grise
et le soleil est jaune.
L'univers est un arc-en-ciel!

THE ALPHABET, IT RHYMES

A, B, C is enough.
D, E, F is too short.
G, H, I is small.
J, K, L is pell-mell.
M, N, O is new.
P, Q, R is great.
S, T, U is well known.
V, W is a dream.
X, Y is Greek.
And the Z is an oddball!
   [*lit.*, a zebra]

THE COLORS OF THE UNIVERSE

The colors of the universe
Planet Earth is blue.
Planet Mars is red.
Planet Jupiter is orange.
The moon is gray
and the sun is yellow.
The universe is a rainbow!

Glossary

Notes
- All French words have a gender. They are either masculine or feminine. The article preceding the noun indicates the gender of the noun: *le* and *un* (the, a) are masculine articles, *la* and *une* are feminine articles. The plural articles are *les* and *des*.
- To form the plural of most nouns, simply add a final "s" to the noun. Some nouns have an irregular plural. In this glossary, irregular plurals are indicated in parentheses (pl.) after the singular noun.
- All adjectives agree in gender and number with the noun they modify. In this glossary, the feminine form of an adjective is indicated in parentheses (f.) after its masculine form.

French–English

A

l'aigle (m.)	eagle
aimer	to love
j'aime	I love
aller	to go
je vais	I'm going, I go
Va!	Go!
l'alphabet (m.)	alphabet
amusant (f. *amusante*)	fun
l'animal (m.) (pl. *les animaux*)	animal
l'antenne (f.)	antenna
s'appeler	to be called
je m'appelle . . .	my name is . . .
tu t'appelles . . .	your name is . . .

◆ DOMESTIC ANIMALS ◆

le canard	duck
le chat	cat
le cheval (pl. *les chevaux*)	horse
le chien	dog
le cochon	pig
le hamster	hamster
le lapin	rabbit
le mouton	sheep
l'oiseau (m.) (pl. *les oiseaux*)	bird
la vache	cow

◆ ◆ WILD ANIMALS ◆ ◆

l'aigle (m.)	eagle
le crocodile	crocodile
le lion	lion
l'ours (m.)	bear
le pingouin	penguin
le requin	shark
le serpent	snake
le tigre	tiger
le zèbre	zebra

applaudir	to applaud
j'applaudis	I applaud
Applaudissez!	Applaud!
l'arbre (m.)	tree
arrêter	to stop
j'arrête	I stop
arrière; en arrière	back(ward), at the back, behind
aujourd'hui	today
aujourd'hui c'est . . .	today is . . .
avancer	to go forward
j'avance	I go forward
l'avion (m.)	airplane
avoir	to have
avoir faim	to be hungry
j'ai faim	I'm hungry
tu as faim	you are hungry

B

le bateau (pl. *les bateaux*)	boat
beau (f. *belle(s)*; pl. *beaux*)	beautiful, pretty
blanc (f. *blanche*)	white
bleu (f. *bleue*)	blue
bonjour	hello, good morning, good afternoon
le bras	arm
le bus	bus

C

le camion	truck
la carte	map
la cassette	cassette
le cerf	deer
la chanson	song
chanter	to sing
je chante	I sing
le chanteur	singer (male)
la chanteuse	singer (female)
le chapeau (pl. *les chapeaux*)	hat

le chat	cat
le cheval (pl. *les chevaux*)	horse
le chien	dog
le clignotant	blinker
commencer	to start
la couleur	color
court (f. *courte*)	short

◆ ◆ ◆ COLORS ◆ ◆ ◆

blanc (f. *blanche*)	white
bleu (f. *bleue*)	blue
gris (f. *grise*)	gray
jaune	yellow
marron (pl. *marron*)	brown
noir (f. *noire*)	black
orange (pl. *orange*)	orange
rose	pink
rouge	red
vert (f. *verte*)	green
violet (f. *violette*)	purple

D

dans	in
danser	to dance
je danse	I dance
Dansez!	Dance!
le désert	desert
le dessert	dessert
dimanche	Sunday
dire	to say
je dis	I say
Jacques a dit . . .	Simon Says . . . (lit., Jack said . . .)
la direction	direction
doubler	to pass (another car)
je double	I am passing (another car)
droit (f. *droite*)	straight
tout droit	straight ahead
la droite	right
à droite	on the right

◆ ◆ ◆ DESSERTS ◆ ◆ ◆

le chocolat	chocolate
le gâteau (pl. *les gâteaux*)	cake
la glace	ice cream

E

l'école (f.)	school
elle (f.)	she, it
elles (f.)	they
ennuyeux (f. ennuyeuse)	boring
étrange	strange, odd
être	to be
je suis	I am
tu es	you are (sing.)
c'est	it's
si j'étais . . .	if I were . . .

F

la faim	hunger
j'ai faim	I'm hungry
la famille	family
le fast-food	fast-food
la fille	girl
la forêt	forest
français (f. française)	French
le français	French language
le frère	brother
le fruit	fruit

G

le garçon	boy
le gâteau	cake
la gauche	left
à gauche	on the left
gentil (f. gentille)	kind, nice
la glace	ice cream
grand (f. grande)	tall, big
gris (f. grise)	gray

H

l'hôtel (m.)	hotel

I

il (m.)	he, it
ils (m.)	they

J

la jambe	leg
jaune	yellow
je	I
le jeu (pl. les jeux)	game
le jeu vidéo (pl. les jeux vidéo)	video game
jeudi	Thursday
le jouet	toy
le jour	day
la jungle	jungle

L

laid (f. laide)	ugly
le légume	vegetable
lent (f. lente)	slow
lever	to raise
je lève	I raise
Levez la bras!	Raise your arm!
Levez la jambe!	Raise your leg!
le lion	lion
le livre	book
long (f. longue)	long
lundi	Monday
les lunettes (f.) de soleil	sunglasses

M

le magasin	shop, store
la maison	house, home
maman	mom
manger	to eat
je mange	I eat
marcher	to walk
je marche	I walk
Marchez!	Walk!
mardi	Tuesday
marron (pl. marron)	brown
mercredi	Wednesday
mettre	to put
je mets	I put on
le clignotant	the blinker
la montagne	mountain
le moteur	engine
le mouchoir	handkerchief
le mouton	sheep
la musique	music

N

la nature	nature
noir (f. noire)	black
non	no
nous	we

O

l'océan (m.)	ocean
l'oiseau (m.)	bird
orange (pl. orange)	orange
oui	yes
l'ours (m.)	bear

P

papa	dad
par	by
le parc	park
petit (f. petite)	small
le phare	headlight
la pièce	coin
la piscine	swimming pool
le plat	dish
la porte	door

Q

quelque chose	something
qui	who, which, that
qui commence par . . .	that starts with . . .

R

ralentir — to slow down
  je ralentis — I slow down
rapide — fast
reculer — to go back
  Reculez! — Go back!
le requin — shark
rose — pink
la roue — wheel
rouge — red

S

samedi — Saturday
sauter — to jump
  Sautez! — Jump!
la semaine — week

◆ FAST-FOOD DISHES ◆

les frites (f.) — French fries
le hamburger — hamburger
le hot dog — hot dog
la pizza — pizza
le taco — taco

le serpent — snake
si — if
la sœur — sister
le stylo — pen

T

le taxi — taxi
tourner — to turn, to make a turn

◆ TRANSPORTATION ◆

l'avion (m.) — airplane
le bateau — boat
  (pl. les bateaux)
le bus — bus
le camion — truck
l'hélicoptère (m.) — helicopter
la jeep — jeep
le métro — subway
la moto — motorcycle
le taxi — taxi
le train — train
le vélo — bicycle
la voiture — car

je tourne — I turn, I make a turn
  Tournez! — Turn!
le trésor — treasure
tu — you (sing. informal)

V

la vache — cow
le véhicule — vehicle
vendredi — Friday
vert (f. verte) — green
la viande — meat
la ville — city
violet (f. violette) — purple
voir — to see
  je vois — I see
la voiture — car
vous — you (plural; sing. formal)
le voyage — trip
  je vais en voyage — I'm going on a trip

Z

le zoo — zoo

English-French

A

airplane	l'avion (m.)
alphabet	l'alphabet (m.)
animal	l'animal (m.; pl. les animaux)
antenna	l'antenne (f.)
to applaud	applaudir
Applaud!	Applaudissez!
arm	le bras

B

back	arrière, en arrière
to be	être
I am	je suis
you are	tu es (sing.); vous êtes (pl.)
it's	c'est
to be called	s'appeler
to be hungry	avoir faim
bear	l'ours (m.)
beautiful, pretty	beau (f. belle; pl. beaux, belles)
big	grand (f. grande)
bird	l'oiseau (m.)
black	noir (f. noire)
blinker	le clignotant
blue	bleu (f. bleue)
boat	le bateau (pl. les bateaux)
book	le livre
boring	ennuyeux (f. ennuyeuse)
boy	le garçon
brother	le frère
brown	marron (pl. marron)
bus	le bus
by	par

✦ ✦ ✦ ✦ CAR ✦ ✦ ✦ ✦

trunk	le coffre
engine	le moteur
windshield	le pare-brise
bumper	le pare-chocs
headlight	le phare
license plate	la plaque d'immatriculation
rearview mirror	le rétroviseur
wheel	la roue
seat	le siège
steering wheel	le volant

C

cake	le gâteau
car	la voiture
cassette	la cassette
cat	le chat
city	la ville
coin	la pièce
color	la couleur
cow	la vache

✦ ✦ ✦ ✦ CITY ✦ ✦ ✦ ✦

movie theater	le cinéma
school	l'école (f.)
hospital	l'hôpital (m.) (pl. les hôpitaux)
hotel	l'hôtel (m.)
shop, store	le magasin
city hall	la mairie
house	la maison
museum	le musée
park	le parc
swimming pool	la piscine
supermarket	le supermarché
zoo	le zoo

D

dad	papa
to dance	danser
Dance!	Dansez!
day	le jour
deer	le cerf
desert	le désert
dessert	le dessert
direction	la direction
dish	le plat
dog	le chien
door	la porte

E

eagle	l'aigle (m.)
to eat	manger
engine	le moteur

F

family	la famille
fast	rapide
fast-food	le fast-food
forest	la forêt
French	français (f. française)
French language	le français
Friday	vendredi
fruit	le fruit
fun	amusant (f. amusante)

G

game	le jeu (pl. les jeux)
video game	le jeu vidéo (pl. les jeux vidéo)
girl	la fille

to go	aller
Go!	Va!
to go back	reculer
Go back!	Reculez!
to go forward	avancer
Go forward!	Avancez!
to go on a trip	aller en voyage
good morning, good afternoon	bonjour
green	vert (f. verte)
gray	gris (f. grise)

H

handkerchief	le mouchoir
hat	le chapeau (pl. les chapeaux)
to have	avoir
I have	j'ai
you have	tu as
he, it (m.)	il
headlight	le phare
hello	bonjour
horse	le cheval (pl. les chevaux)
hotel	l'hôtel (m.)
house, home	la maison
hunger	la faim
to be hungry	avoir faim

I

I	je
ice cream	la glace
if	si
if I were . . .	si j'étais . . .
in	dans
it's	c'est

✦ ✦ ✦ ✦ MUSIC ✦ ✦ ✦ ✦

cassette	la cassette
song	la chanson
singer	le chanteur/ la chanteuse
radio	la radio
walkman	le walkman

J

to jump	sauter
Jump!	Sautez!
jungle	la jungle

L

left	la gauche
to the left	à gauche
leg	la jambe
lion	le lion
long	long (f. longue)
to love	aimer
I love	j'aime

M

map	*la carte*
meat	*la viande*
mom	*maman*
Monday	*lundi*
mountain	*la montagne*
My name is . . .	*Je m'appelle . . .*

✦ ✦ ✦ ✦ MEATS ✦ ✦ ✦ ✦

turkey	*la dinde*
chicken	*le poulet*
sausage	*la saucisse*
steak	*le steak*

N

name	*le nom*
My name is . . .	*Je m'appelle . . .*
nature	*la nature*
no	*non*

O

ocean	*l'océan* (m.)
odd	*étrange*
orange	*orange* (pl. *orange*)

P

park	*le parc*
to pass (another car)	*doubler*
pen	*le stylo*
pink	*rose*
purple	*violet* (f. *violette*)
to put	*mettre*
I put	*je mets*
to put on the blinker	*mettre le clignotant*
to raise	*lever*
Raise!/Lift!	*Levez!*
red	*rouge*
right	*la droite*
to the right	*à droite*

S

Saturday	*samedi*
to say	*dire*
I say	*je dis*
Simon says . . .	*Jacques a dit . . .*
school	*l'école* (f.)
to see	*voir*
I see	*je vois*
shark	*le requin*
she, it *(f.)*	*elle*
sheep	*le mouton*
shop, store	*le magasin*
short	*court* (f. *courte*)
to sing	*chanter*
I sing	*je chante*
singer	*le chanteur/la chanteuse*
sister	*la sœur*
slow	*lent* (f. *lente*)
to slow down	*ralentir*
I slow down	*je ralentis*
you slow down	*tu ralentis*
small	*petit* (f. *petite*)
snake	*le serpent*
something	*quelque chose*
song	*la chanson*
to start	*commencer*
that starts with . . .	*qui commence par . . .*
steering wheel	*le volant*
to stop	*arrêter*
I stop	*j'arrête*
you stop	*tu arrêtes*
straight	*droit* (f. *droite*)
straight ahead	*tout droit*
strange	*étrange*
Sunday	*dimanche*
sunglasses	*les lunettes* (f.) *de soleil*
swimming pool	*la piscine*

T

tall	*grand* (f. *grande*)
taxi	*le taxi*
that	*qui, que*
they	*elles* (f.); *ils* (m.)
Thursday	*jeudi*
today	*aujourd'hui*
Today is . . .	*Aujourd'hui c'est . . .*
toy	*le jouet*
treasure	*le trésor*

tree	*l'arbre* (m.)
trip	*le voyage*
truck	*le camion*
Tuesday	*mardi*
to turn	*tourner*
Turn!	*Tournez!*
to make a turn	*tourner*
I make a turn	*je tourne*

U

ugly	*laid* (f. *laide*)

V

vegetable	*le légume*
vehicle	*le véhicule*
video game	*le jeu vidéo* (pl. *les jeux vidéo*)

✦ ✦ ✦ VEGETABLES ✦ ✦ ✦

broccoli	*le brocoli*
carrot	*la carotte*
green bean	*le haricot vert*
potato	*la pomme de terre*
tomato	*la tomate*

W

to walk	*marcher*
Walk!	*Marchez!*
we	*nous*
Wednesday	*mercredi*
week	*la semaine*
wheel	*la roue*
white	*blanc* (f. *blanche*)
who	*qui*

Y

yellow	*jaune*
yes	*oui*
you	*vous* (pl.; sing. formal), *tu* (sing. informal)

Z

zoo	*le zoo*

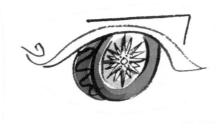

la montagne

Lundi

Mardi

Mercredi

Jeudi

Vendredi

Samedi

Dimanche

P G A H E

W O T V R

vert

rouge

jaune

bleu

l'océan

l'arbre

la forêt

la vache

le cheval

l'oiseau

le mouton

le chien

la jungle